W9-BIM-865

Queenston Dr. P. S.

Larry
the loon

Judith McMurray

Illustrated by D. A. Dunford

with

The Tobin Island School of Fine Art
Loretta Rogers
Darcey Sills
Karen Genovese
Susan Gosevitz
Dwight Aranha
Simon Dunford, Junior Member
Megan Torisawa, Junior Member

Foreword and Art by Robert Bateman, Guest Artist, Andy Donato

Text copyright © 2011 Judith McMurray
Illustrations copyright © 2011 D. A. Dunford,
© 2011 Robert Bateman, © 2011 Andy Donato,
© 2011 The Tobin Island School of Fine Art with
Simon Dunford and Megan Torisawa
Photography © 2011 Turnbull Photography

All rights reserved. No part of this publication may be reproduced or
transmitted in any form or by any means, electronic or mechanical,
including photocopying, recording, or any information storage and
retrieval system, without permission in writing from the publisher.

Edited and designed by Cynthia McMurray,
Photography by Scott Turnbull
Printed and bound in Canada at Friesens

Library and Archives Canada Cataloguing in Publication

McMurray, Judith
    Larry the loon / Judith McMurray; illustrated by D.A.
Dunford ; with the Tobin Island School of Fine Art.

ISBN 978-1-927003-05-3

    1. Loons--Juvenile fiction. I. Dunford, Doug, 1953- II. Tobin Island School of Fine Art (Toronto,
Ont.) III. Title.

PS8625.M875L37 2011   jC813'.6   C2011-902327-X

10 9 8 7 6 5 4 3 2 1

Published in 2011 by Bryler Publications Inc.
Little Fish Books
Box 1035,
Chester, NS
B0J 1J0

www.brylerpublications.com

ENVIRONMENTAL BENEFITS STATEMENT

Bryler Publications saved the following resources by printing the pages of this book on chlorine free paper made with 10% post-consumer waste.

TREES	WATER	ENERGY	SOLID WASTE	GREENHOUSE GASES
3	**1,040**	**1**	**66**	**230**
FULLY GROWN	GALLONS	MILLION BTUs	POUNDS	POUNDS

Environmental impact estimates were made using the Environmental Paper Network Paper Calculator. For more information visit www.papercalculator.org.

little fish
BOOKS

For
Hailey and Blake
Our Treasured Twosome

Robert Bateman, Northern Reflections - Loon Family, 24" x 36", oil, 1981

Photography by Birgit Freybe

The Canadian Wildlife Federation (CWF)

CANADIAN   FÉDÉRATION
WILDLIFE   CANADIENNE
FEDERATION DE LA FAUNE

The Canadian Wildlife Federation (CWF) is a national charitable organization dedicated to wildlife conservation and education. Representing over 300,000 supporters across Canada, CWF works from coast to coast to maintain something very important — a bright future for Canada's wildlife.

Canada is blessed with an abundance of nature. No matter where you live in the country, wildlife is always close by. Canadians care deeply about ensuring that our rich heritage of diverse wildlife is conserved. CWF empowers Canadians to help protect wild species and the spaces they call home through beautiful publications, award-winning programs and a balanced approach to wildlife issues. Since our inception in 1962, we've become a household name because of our leadership in conservation education, awareness and outreach.

CWF knows how vital it is that wildlife and the environment still hold a place in everyone's hearts. We know we can't do it alone, but we also know that together we are making a difference. With the support of individuals and organizations like Children's Books for Charity, Judith McMurray, author of *Larry the Loon,* and Bryler Publications, CWF continues to provide a voice for wildlife.

To find out more about CWF and our programs, visit CanadianWildlifeFederation.ca.

Loretta Rogers, 2011

Foreword

If I think about the best symbol for the Canadian wild, it would be the common loon. The map of the distribution of the common loon is virtually the map of Canada. Some of my earliest memories are at the age of eight, lying in bed at our summer cottage and listening to the call of the loon. Our cottage was on a large lake in Haliburton County in the Canadian Shield. To me, this was Canada's mystic north. In those days, the sound of a motor, especially at night, was a rare thing. The long, yodelling cry of the loon would echo between the shores and my heart would almost stand still. Then there would be the lilting laughter. When this happened in flight, we thought that it was a prediction of rain.

Loons are part of this wonderful northern package of clean waters, spruce and pine and precambrian rocks, as pure and eternal as all of nature.

Of course, in nature, no condition is permanent and I have seen a steady decline in that purity. Forests are being over cut and the lakes are being polluted by too much and too careless human influence. Motor boats are especially damaging. Loons usually nest in sheltered waters where large wave action has never occurred. Because they can hardly walk on land, their nests must be right at the water's edge. If a careless boater zooms in too close to the sheltered nest, it produces a wave that can wash the eggs into the water. This "vroom vroom" mentality, as I like to call it— speed for the sake of "fun"— is very destructive and something I feel very strongly against. Usually, the damage to loons by fast motor boats is merely thoughtless, and not done on purpose. Once, however, when my brother and I were sitting on the dock at our cottage, we heard the distress call of the loons. There was a pair with babies far out on the lake with a couple of teenagers in a fast boat, circling back and forth, trying to run over the birds. Since we did not have a motor boat, we jumped in our canoe to paddle out and put a stop to the madness. It was a long paddle but before we reached a quarter of the way, four different motor boats had raced out from other cottages and confronted the heartless boys. I hope those kids will never forget that bawling out.

Thank goodness there is now much more awareness of the preciousness of the loons and indeed, all of nature. I somehow have faith that our grandchildren's grandchildren will still have loons to wonder over as I have done all my life.

This book captures the beauty of loons and the poignancy of their relationship with humans.

Robert Bateman

Susan Gosevitz 2011

Larry the loon was a proud new father.

He watched his chick peck through its thick speckled shell and emerge wide eyed into the world.

The tiny bird, covered in a wet down, pulled itself free using its small black beak and large webbed feet.

Susan Gosevitz 2011

As soon as its downy feathers were dry and fluffy, Larry sank low into the cold, late spring water so the newborn could hop on his back. Larry raised his large wings slightly to cradle the baby.

Then, mother and father loon took their chick for its first view of the glistening deep blue lake in Northern Canada.

When the family returned to the shoreline, Larry again lowered himself in the water so the baby could jump off. Mother loon made sure the baby was safely back in its large nest made of cattail reeds and grasses then covered it with her wing to keep it warm.

Knowing his family would be hungry soon, Larry ventured back out on the dark water to find food. The sun's warm rays glistened off the tiny water droplets on Larry's beautiful black and white feathers, which formed a unique pattern of checks, stripes and dots. His red eyes glowed in the morning sunshine.

D. A. Dunford 2011

When he found the perfect spot, Larry began to swim in circles, waiting patiently to dive for the tasty fish just below the surface. His stomach growled and his long, POINTED black beak quivered in anticipation of his first fish of the day.

"Aha," Larry said, as he glimpsed a small rock bass swimming by.

"I see dinner."

Darcey Sills 2011

He quickly pulled his wings in close to his body and prepared to dive. Like all loons, Larry had powerful webbed feet, which he used to propel himself deep below the surface. He could dive up to 200 feet and hold his breath for almost three minutes before he needed to come up for air.

Larry was also a very fast swimmer. He used his sleek body to submarine through the cold, deep waters. He kept his long webbed toes open on the backstroke and then expertly folded them up tightly on the forward stroke, making him fast enough to catch almost any fish in the lake.

Loretta Rogers 2011

Loretta Rogers
2011

Susan Gosevitz 2011

Right now, he had his eye on the little rock bass still darting back and forth below him.

He suddenly felt the calm water vibrate and then he heard a thunderous noise. He turned toward the middle of the lake just in time to see a flash of red, as a large motor boat sliced through the waves.

The boat was racing straight toward him.

Larry was an expert diver. He knew he could quickly **duck** below the motor boat before it hit him, but as he stuck his big webbed feet out of the water they got tangled in a mass of floating weeds drifting on the surface.

It was too late!

 D. A. Dunford 2011

D.A.Dunford 2011

In a split second, Larry was hit by the speeding boat and his feathery body flew up into the air before hitting the water.

Poor Larry came down hard and he hurt all over. His body shook from the impact. Larry was very frightened but he knew he needed to get home. He tried to move his feet so he could paddle back to shore and his family but only one of his feet worked. He swam in circles, like a row boat with only one oar.

Only one of his wings would move. Poor Larry was a real mess. The motor boat was now out of sight and he was alone. The lake where he had spent many seasons, swimming and catching fish, suddenly looked very big.

Karen Genovese 2011

Susan Gosevitz 2011

D.A. Dunford 2011

After many attempts, Larry finally used his uninjured foot to paddle himself into a sheltered bay. Nestled among the cattails, Larry tucked his head under his perfectly spotted wing and cried the chilling, soulful cry of the loon.

He wasn't aware of the family sitting on a dock in the small bay. They had been watching Larry struggling to reach safety in the shallow waters. Loons are solitary birds. They are very shy and frighten easily, so they seldom come near people.

"Mom, Dad, come quick. I think that loon is in trouble. Listen to him cry," a small girl called to her parents.

"I think you're right," her father said, squinting into the bright sun to see the bird.

Larry was drifting toward them now. The father gently put his hand into the water and offered Larry a bite of the salmon he had been eating. Larry was starving. He had not eaten since yesterday morning. He opened his beak and carefully took the piece of fish. It tasted so good. The father leaned closer to the injured bird and offered him more salmon. Larry eagerly opened his beak.

D. A. Dunford 2011

D.A. Dunford

Early the next morning, the family came back to check on Larry. The tired loon hadn't flown away. He was still floating near the dock and he looked very hungry and frightened. Once again, the father fed Larry some small pieces of fish. Larry was very grateful for the food. Loons need to eat almost two pounds of fish every day just to stay healthy and in the past two days, Larry had only eaten two small pieces of salmon. Now that Larry was hurt, he couldn't feed himself as he was unable to dive for fish.

Every day for the next few weeks, the family took turns making sure Larry got enough food. They fed him pickled herring, **CRAB** legs and fresh salmon. The children even caught rock bass and lake trout for Larry. As the days passed, the family hoped Larry would feel better and go on his way, but it wasn't to be.

Darcey Sills 2011

"I think we need to take Larry to a wildlife rescue center," the father told his family, after weeks of feeding Larry with no signs of improvement.

"It will be fall soon, and loons fly south for the winter," the father explained to his children. "Loons run on the water to take off and with his injuries, I'm not sure this poor loon will be able to fly. If he stays here, he will likely freeze. The nights are already getting colder."

The little girl looked at Larry. He seemed very sad, floating in the shallow bay all by himself.

"How will we get him to the rescue center?" she asked.

Father pointed to a small fishing boat tied to the other side of the long dock. He asked the children to join him and they rowed the little boat over to Larry, who was floating just a few feet from the shore now.

Larry looked up at them with his sad red eyes. He was not afraid. He knew the family was trying to help him. Father gently scooped Larry up in his large fishing net. Loons have a small oil-filled sac just below their tails. When they preen, they use this water-proof oil to coat their feathers, which keeps them smooth and warm in the colder weather. His sleek body easily slid into the net. The father gently held Larry's wings closed and then carefully placed him into a **cardboard** box with a small hole so he could breathe. After they docked the boat, the family quickly put Larry into the car and drove him to the wildlife rescue center.

Simon Dunford 2010, age 15

A tall green sign with red and white letters stood at the entrance to the centre. The station wagon pulled up to a large building with a green shingled roof. The father gently lifted the box out of the car and carried Larry into the centre, where the family waited anxiously to see a veterinarian.

It didn't take long for a very nice man with grey hair and a big moustache to welcome them into an examining room.

"I'm Doctor Bernie," he said, carefully examining Larry. After several minutes, he looked up over his big wire-rimmed glasses and sighed.

"Oh dear. This little guy looks badly injured."

"Can you help him?" the father asked.

"I will try." The doctor took the box from the father. Larry's long beak was sticking out of the hole. He looked very tired and sad but the doctor promised to do his best to help him.

A few days went by before the family heard from the doctor. They had just about given up hope, worried Larry may have been too injured to survive, when they finally received a call asking them to come to the wildlife center.

The children were very excited. When they opened the door to the rehabilitation room they saw Larry splashing around in a large tub filled with water lilies. He had a splint on one wing and a cast on his injured foot.

"In about one month, I will remove the splints and then you can watch as we release Larry back into the lake," the doctor said. "This loon is very lucky that you found him and brought him here. Most birds that are hit by speeding boats aren't as lucky." He sighed. "I wish boaters would be more careful on the water."

Larry opened his beak and made a loud loon call.

"That must be 'thank you' in loon talk," said the daughter. Everyone laughed.

D. A. Dunford 2011

The next summer, the family returned to the lake. As they made their way down to the long dock overlooking the shallow bay, they heard a familiar call.

"Look Dad," the little girl said, pointing to a small **alcove** on the other side of the fishing boat. "It's Larry!"

"Well, will you look at that," the father said, stretching to see across the bay. "I think you're right . . . and he's not alone," he added.

Perched happily on Larry's back was a small chick. Its thick, downy black feathers stood out in the late afternoon sun. The mother loon led the family into the shallow bay.

"Larry must have found his mate." The father smiled, watching Larry proudly carry his new chick around the small lagoon. "Loons often mate for life, you know."

"And, thanks to you, this family of loons will be safe here now," the mother said, looking proudly at her own children.

Loretta Rogers 2011

After Larry's accident the two children started a petition to enforce safe boating on their lake. All of their neighbours were so touched by Larry's story that they all agreed to be more aware of the wildlife on the lake.

The children giggled as they watched Larry and his family paddle across the water.

"I think we should call that one Larry Junior," the little girl said, pointing to the baby riding on Larry' back.

"I think you're right again," the father said.

And from that day on, all loons lived safely on that glistening deep blue lake in Northern Canada.

Did you Know?

- Loons have been around for up to 50-million years!
- Loons can live up to 30 years.
- Loons are larger than ducks but smaller than geese and can grow up to 3-feet long and weigh between 8 and 12 pounds. The male is usually larger than the female.
- The common loon has a black bill, head and neck with distinctive white stripes, checks and spots on their backs. They have brilliant red eyes, which help them see underwater. Their feathers change colour in the winter. A brownish grey coat means they are not breeding.
- Loons have solid bones. This extra weight helps them dive as deep as 200 feet.
- Loons can fly up to 72-miles per hour.
- Loons need a long distance to gain speed for take-off on water. They are also very clumsy on land because their legs are positioned at the rear of their bodies.
- When a loon is scared or feels threatened, it will fold its wings against its body and rear up. This is called a "penguin dance" because it is similar to how a penguin moves. This is very tiring for a loon, so you should never startle them or get too close because they can actually die from exhaustion.
- Both the male and female loons build the nest using reeds and grasses. They do not breed until they are three-or four-years old.
- The female loon usually lays one or two eggs, which hatch in 28 to 30 days. The babies leave the nest on the first day they are born and the parents carry them on their backs to protect them from turtles, fish and even raccoons, weasels and skunks. The babies are not able to fly until they are 2-months old, at which time they can feed on their own.
- In September, loons travel to Florida or the Gulf of Mexico for the winter. In April, they are seen back on the northern lakes in Canada.
- Loons are best known for their yodel, hoot, wail and tremolo calls. Their calls have been called haunting, beautiful, thrilling, mystical and enchanting.
- Loons hunt by swimming, using their webbed feet to propel them through the water. They eat small fish, crayfish and even frogs and insects.
- The common loon is also known as the Great Northern Diver.
- Loons have few predators, but bald eagles and osprey have been known to attack them on occasion.

Alternate Ending

While this additional ending is the true story of what happened
to Larry the Loon, it may not be suitable for all ages.
Parents should read this version of the ending first and then
make a decision as to whether their child is ready to learn about
compassionate euthanasia. Although the story is written in such
a way as to help teach children that sometimes, helping an
animal involves doing what is truly best for them, it still
may be disturbing for some readers.

We will leave this decision up to you. Should you not want to
expose your child to this issue just yet, this ending can
easily be removed using the perforated pages.

Whatever ending you chose to read to your child, we hope to
show that conscientious and responsible boating and treatment
of our environment is imperative if we are to continue to coexist
with the many amazing and beautiful
species on our planet.

— *The Author and Illustrators*

The ride to the wildlife centre was quiet. Everyone was very worried about Larry. They knew his injuries were bad—with a broken wing and foot, he could not fly or feed himself.

Father finally broke the silence, "I know we are all hoping Larry will make a full recovery and return to the lake... but he is hurt pretty badly."

He turned to look at Larry who had stuck his head out of the cardboard box that was sitting between the two children in the back seat. His deep red eyes looked tired and scared and the father knew the loon was in pain.

"The doctors will try their best to help him," the father added, sighing loudly.

"We know," the little girl said. "We just don't want Larry to suffer anymore than he already has. We want what is best for him."

A tall green sign with red and white letters stood at the entrance to the wildlife centre. The station wagon pulled up to a large building with a green shingled roof. The father gently lifted the box out of the car and carried Larry into the centre, where the family waited anxiously to see the vet. It didn't take long for a very nice man with grey hair and big moustache to welcome them into an examining room.

"I'm Doctor Bernie," he said, carefully examining Larry. After several minutes, he looked up over his big wire rimmed glasses and sighed. "This loon's foot is badly crushed. I'm not sure we can fix it." He turned to the mother and father. "His wing is also badly broken. Larry won't be able to catch fish to feed himself."

He then looked at the children and lowered his voice until he was speaking very softly, "I will give Larry some medicine and he will fall asleep. This is a gentle and kind way to help an injured animal. When Larry

wakes up, he will be in heaven, free of all his pain and he will be much happier."
The children turned to their parents, and then they all looked at Larry. He seemed weak and tired. He had tried very hard to get better but the injuries caused by the boat were just too serious.

The family all agreed. They knew they had to do what was best for Larry.

"I'm glad we took all those pictures of Larry" the daughter said. "I will always remember him."

The family took a few moments to pat Larry's sleek black head and the daughter gave him the last salmon treat she had hidden in her pocket. He looked at her then gobbled it down.

That afternoon, when the family returned to their cottage, the children gathered all the pictures they had of Larry and placed them in a small photo album.

"I miss Larry," the little girl said, holding a picture of the injured loon as he ate a big piece of fish.

"Me too," said the father, placing his hand on her shoulder.

"I think we should tell people about Larry. Maybe, if they knew Larry, they would be more careful on the lake."

"I think that's a great idea," the father said.

So, after dinner, the mother and father and the two children visited all of their neighbours on the lake. They brought the photo album filled with beautiful pictures of Larry and told everyone about how they found the poor bird, hurt and alone in the bay. They explained how helpless he was and that he could not feed himself because of his injuries. The children reminded their neighbours that loons and other wildlife live on the lake and that boaters must be more careful so another bird like Larry is never hurt again. The neighbours were so touched by Larry's story that they all promised to be more careful.

As the family made their way back to the cottage, they heard a familiar sound coming from the shallow bay near their dock. The children ran toward the water.

"Come quick," the little girl called to her parents. "Look!"

There, in the small inlet, was a mother loon and her chick. Water droplets on its downy black feathers, glistened in the light of the bright orange sunset. The pair splashed about in the water as the baby loon tried to keep up with his mother.

"He reminds me of Larry," the little girl said. "I'm going to call the baby Larry Jr.," she announced. "And now, that everyone knows to be careful on the water, he will grow up to look just like him," she added.

Everyone smiled as Larry Jr. hopped on his mother's back and the two loons made their way to their nest.

D. A. Dunford 2010